For Seth Duey

X-MEN™
ULTIMATE PICTURE BOOK

Published by

BIG GUY BOOKS®
www.bigguybooks.com

www.marvel.com

Director & Photographer	3D & Special Effects Digital Illustrator	Writer	Story Boards, Casting, Costume Design
ROBERT GOULD	**EUGENE EPSTEIN**	**KATHLEEN DUEY**	**RAIN RAMOS**

Based on characters created by Stan Lee, Jack Kirby, Mark Miller, Adam Kubert and Andy Kubert.

Dateline: Washington, D.C. 9:00 PM EST:

"This hour's top story: Human genes are changing, mutating. Some mutants are easy to spot; others aren't, but one thing is clear: All of them have powers that threaten civilization as we know it...."

"The president's Sentinel program is finally complete. The gigantic robots are designed to detect mutant genes—then to destroy the mutants themselves. Government sources are confident the Sentinels can eliminate the Mutant Brotherhood and its

LIVE

**WAR
ON
MUTANTS**

7 news

7 news

VOTES · UNICARE ▲ · NAS ▼19.11

I'm Ororo Monroe. Weird name, isn't it? People back home sure thought so. The X-Men have given me a new name: Storm. It fits. I can generate *lightning!*

My power accidentally got me into trouble. Then Jean found me. Her telepathy is amazing. She made the sheriff think she was a 40-year-old police detective so he would release me.

I am Piotr Rasputin. I am from Siberia. Things are terrible there—people are starving. To support my family, I became involved with international gangs. I am ashamed of this now,

but back then, it seemed like I had no choice. I hid my powers, of course. Every mutant learns to do this. Then one day, it all went wrong.

The deal went bad and the helicopter opened fire. I changed my flesh into metal to save myself. I had to reveal my mutant powers—or die.

The Sentinel program is worldwide—I was sure I'd see robots overhead any second. Then Jean Grey appeared. She read my thoughts; she knew how desperate I was. I am called Colossus.

The Sentinel attacks terrify mutants everywhere. Magneto has built a fortress city on a remote island. He is convinced: Mutants must rid the Earth of normal humans in order to survive. But at Professor Xavier's

For the first time in his life, Beast didn't feel like a freak walking down the hall. This school *was* different. None of them would have to hide their powers here.

The marble floor was smooth as glass. The place looked like a billionaire's mansion, not a school. Jean Grey introduced everyone, then briefed them on their way to the library. "There's a reason for everything," she explained. "The costume fabric hides our mutant genes from the Sentinels. The nicknames protect our families—"

"You'll learn to develop and control your powers here," Cyclops added. "Our technology is amazing. The communication headsets, our jet, and…"

"…and here's the library," Jean interrupted. She led them forward. "Professor? They're here. Beast, Storm, Colossus…this is Professor Charles Xavier."

"Professor Xavier was paralyzed in a battle with Magneto years ago," Jean whispered.

Beast stared. The man's eyes were as piercing and direct as a laser. He didn't speak. He sent his thoughts directly into their minds.

"Welcome. Thank you for coming, for trusting me. You are X-Men now. In my school, you will work to master your powers. You will learn to use them to help humanity—all of humanity."

"The helmet is part of a machine called Cerebro," Jean whispered. "It magnifies his powers. He found all of you like this."

"I hope you won't mind working your first day here A boy named Bobby Drake is in trouble, running away from home to protect his family from Sentinels."

Bobby Drake could hear his own heartbeat over the noise of the bus. He knew the Sentinels would find him soon.

Colossus stepped forward. "I am ready."
One by one, the others nodded. They had spent their lives running; they all knew how it felt.
Cyclops spoke up. "Where is he, Professor?"

Downtown was crowded; people stared at the X-Men. Jean spotted Bobby Drake cowering in the back of the bus. Beast tore open the emergency door and grabbed the boy—the Sentinels only a split second behind.

An explosion rocked the street, rolling the bus. Beast smashed his way out, Bobby barely managing to hang on. The poor kid was terrified. Beast understood. The Sentinels were like a nightmare...but there was no way to wake up.

The pavement shook. Buildings trembled. People were screaming, shoving each other, desperate to get out of the way. Only the X-Men stood their ground.

Cyclops directed the battle. The Sentinels were deadly—and the X-Men fought for their lives.

Storm created a massive lightning bolt, destroying the robots' microneuroprocessors. Without guidance systems, three of the Sentinels went down *hard*. Cyclops took out a fourth, then hesitated, afraid of hurting onlookers. He opened his communications channel. "X-Men! Clear the area!"

All around Bobby, people were running, terrified. Their fear snapped him out of his own. He summoned his powers and raised his hands.

"Get down!" Bobby shouted, letting the strange force flow from his fingertips. The supernatural cold hit the Sentinel and in seconds, the robot was coated in tons of ice, frozen in place.

The crowd was stunned into silence, then a man shook his fist. People shifted, glaring. "Lousy mutants!" someone screamed. "Hey, freak! Ice man!" A bottle hurtled through the air. "Look out!" Cyclops shouted. Bobby turned,

"Call the Sentinel alert line!" a woman shouted. "They're mutants!"
Bobby felt sick. What was *with* these people?

The Sentinels had started the fight in a crowded street. The X-Men had saved the life of every single person there.

But none of that mattered.

The news reached Magneto's island in seconds. He wasn't surprised. His brother had been teaching mutants to live in peace with inferior humans for years. Ridiculous! It was time to get rid of him. But how? Xavier could read minds.

Magneto adjusted the helmet that protected him from Xavier's telepathy—and began to form a plan. Who could be trusted with this? Quicksilver? No. Magneto knew his son wasn't strong enough. Toad? Blob? The Scarlet Witch?

None of his followers would be able to eliminate Xavier. There had to be a way...*WOLVERINE.* He almost smiled. Perfect. He'd lay a trap with Wolverine as bait. The X-Men wouldn't be able to resist saving another mutant in trouble.

In another city, two nights later, Wolverine was leaving his apartment when he sensed danger, but it was already too late. The net was heavy and the first jolt of electricity knocked him backward. He could hear men's voices.

"Watch it! He's dangerous!"
"Don't touch that net. You'll get fried!"
"What about him?"
"Don't worry about him. He heals in minutes, the stinkin' mutant!"

Wolverine slashed at the net, but the enormous voltage coursing through his metal-reinforced bones weakened him, dragging him into unconsciousness.

Professor Xavier watched Cerebro's screens with the X-Men, his face grim.

"They'll torture him again." Professor Xavier shook his head. "Magneto's hatred of humans will start making sense to him sooner or later."

Beast frowned. "We should help him."

Professor Xavier nodded. "We don't want him as an enemy if we can prevent it."

Storm stared at the screen. "Who *is* this guy?"

Professor Xavier met her eyes. "The most dangerous mutant in the world. Wolverine."

Wolverine couldn't escape. The cage had to be adamantium—the same metal that made his bones indestructible. Something

caught his attention. A black aircraft hovered just above the street as six strangely dressed people jumped to the ground.

A guy with weird sunglasses shouted orders while a metal giant tore off the door. There were heavy footsteps overhead. Wolverine glanced upward. Had to be another mutant—who else would have size 45 feet?
But what were they all doing here?

I'm Jean Grey, a sweet voice said inside his mind. Wolverine turned. She was beautiful.
She winked at him. *Welcome to the X-Men, honey.*

Dateline: Washington, D.C. 8:00 PM EST "The nation is stunned tonight. The president's daughter has been kid–napped. The mutant Magneto has claimed responsibility. He's demanding an end to the Sentinel attacks."

Professor Xavier was gravely concerned. *"People will want revenge on all mutants for this. That girl must be saved."*

Jean caught Wolverine's attention. He nodded.

Truth was, he liked the X-Men more than he'd ever liked anyone in his whole lonely life. Maybe trying to live in peace with normal people *was* the right thing to do.

Professor Xavier had used Cerebro to locate the girl. The president's daughter was exhausted and scared.

Quicksilver wasn't as bad as the others. He acted like he felt sorry for her, but he kept glancing around like he was afraid Magneto might still be watching.

Magneto had brought her here, then left her alone with these...creatures. They were all so strange, so creepy....

Toad grimaced suddenly. "The X-Men are here!" Scarlet Witch laughed. "Get real, Toad. No one can find us here. The nearest town is 30 miles away!"

An instant later, they heard Blackbird landing. But it was too late.

The battle exploded. The president's daughter pressed against the wall, too scared to try to escape. "Get the girl," a man with knives sticking out of his hands shouted.

A mutant with huge feet turned and looked at her. A second later he grabbed her and headed for the door. "Don't worry," he told her. "We're here to take you home. We're the good guys."

Wolverine hot-wired one of Magneto's Ferraris. Beast carried the girl carefully—the poor kid was in shock—

Wolverine knew it wasn't going to be easy. It was going to be close.

Jean's telepathic thoughts came into his mind as he drove and she explained her plan.

Blackbird will be in position.. trust me

and got her safely into the car. Wolverine put the car in gear and took off.

"So all I have to do is get this thing up to 120 and drive it straight off a cliff?" he asked sarcastically.

If you can get past Scarlet Witch...

Wolverine grinned. "See you in a minute."

He put the gas pedal to the floor.

Wolverine glanced at the girl. "Hang on!" Suddenly, the car hurtled off the dirt road and into the air. Blackbird swooped toward them. Wolverine felt the car fall, then rise when it should have kept falling. He could feel Jean straining, struggling to focus her mental powers to save the girl, to save *him*.

Wolverine sat still, helpless to do anything but rely on his friends. *Friends.* The word felt out of place inside his tough-guy skull—but it felt good.

They slammed into the cargohold, with a jarring impact. The girl screamed. Blackbird trembled, then steadied.

Wolverine jerked his foot off the gas as the air bags deployed. It took a second for him to believe

As the cargo door began to close, he glanced back... this battle wasn't over.

Storm hurled lightning bolts at Magneto. He barely seemed to notice. Cyclops sent a strong laser blast. Magneto deflected it with a gesture of his hand.

In a blur, Quicksilver hurtled past, then slowed, looking back to see if his father was watching. He wasn't. Magneto simply stood calmly, staring into the distance.

"Look out!" Cyclops shouted.
Toad and Blob were coming at them, their faces distorted in anger. Storm braced herself and let the electricity flow from her fingertips. Iceman backed her up, his weird supercold blasts immobilizing the attackers.

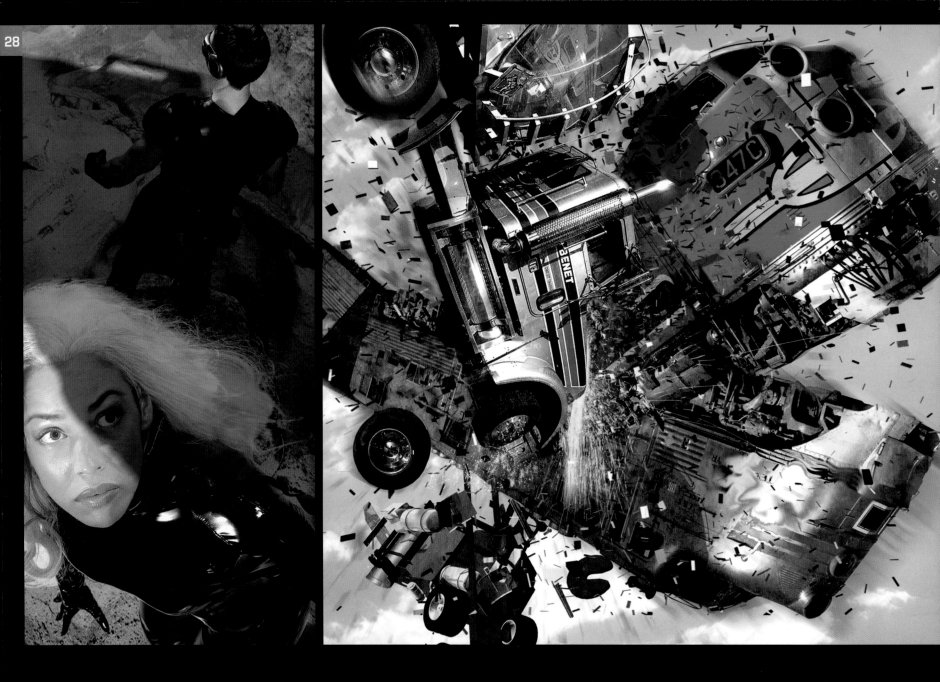

Storm heard a rasping, metallic squeal. She looked up. Magneto had used his powers to pick up...*a whole train? And that wasn't all.*

Magneto's rage had amplified his power. The train's engine weighed 70 tons. The truck was almost as heavy. Perfect. He brought them closer...closer....

Tons of metal crashed to the Earth. The X-Men had no time to react. The ground seemed to lurch upward, then collapse again. Storm dropped into a crouch to keep her balance. Then she stood upright, astonished. "He could have killed us! All of us! But he—"

An explosion in the smoking heap of ruined metal cut off her words.

Cyclops faced a sudden wall of flame, stunned.
Magneto appeared, walking through the fire,
his face hard as stone. "What are you doing?
Saving the daughter of a man who hates you,
me, and every mutant in the world? *Why?*"
Cyclops tried to come up with an answer. He
couldn't. It made sense in a way.

"Why fight mutants?" Magneto demanded.
"It's the normal humans we have to defeat!"
Cyclops stared. Magneto was right. It was
pointless to battle each other.
"Take the girl," Magneto said. "It won't
matter—the president's Sentinels will keep
hunting us."
He turned his back on them in disgust.

Cyclops thought about it for days. He read newspaper articles about Sentinel attacks nationwide. He paced the hallways. Then he finally admitted it to himself: Magneto was right. The only way to defeat power was with greater power.

"I have to leave," Cyclops told the professor. He was stunned. "I'm asking you to reconsider."

Cyclops shook his head. "I'm sick of watching mutants die and…"

"But If the X-Men can convince people that…"

"But we can't!" Cyclops exploded. "Magneto's force is growing because he's right! The only way to survive is to fight back." Before Professor Xavier could answer, Cyclops turned and walked out.

Not long after that, on the remote island of the Mutant Brotherhood...

For the first few days, Cyclops watched Magneto's reactions. The mutant leader seemed glad to have him there—they all did—except Quicksilver.

Magneto's son was the only one who remained distant, who seemed angry that Cyclops had left the X-Men to join Magneto's force.

As the days passed, Cyclops began to understand why. Magneto was a great leader, but he was a lousy father. When he wasn't criticizing Quicksilver, he ignored him.

At first it was exciting. There were hundreds of details involved in the Mutant Brotherhood's attack plans. They wanted to destroy an old castle outside Frankfurt, Germany—it was being converted into a Sentinel base. People needed to realize that the Sentinel program was wrong, that mutants were human beings, too.

But once the building had been destroyed, Cyclops felt terrible—innocent people had been injured. He could tell that Quicksilver was sorry, but it was clear that Magneto didn't care, so long as the attack was successful.

Cyclops knew Professor Xavier would never have allowed something like this to happen.

The president was grateful to have his daughter back, but Professor Xavier couldn't convince him not to attack Magneto's fortress city.

Wolverine watched the professor react to the decision. He was trying desperately to contact Cyclops—they all knew he was probably still on Magneto's island. If the Sentinels attacked, Cyclops would be killed, along with the rest of Magneto's force.

The roaring of the Sentinels' rockets shook the building. No one on the president's task force seemed to notice.

Out on the streets, people glanced up, but no one stopped to stare anymore. They were all used to it.

Magneto rewrote the Sentinels' program code. With the directives of their computer systems rearranged, they would now hunt for humans *without* mutant —and they would begin their mission in Washington D.C.

"What are you doing?" Cyclops demanded. "Where are you sending them?"

"I won't let them destroy the whole world." Magneto shouted over the roar of the robots taking off, "just the city that sent them to me!"

As Cyclops stared at the monstrous robots streaking away—toward his friends, toward millions of innocent people—the magnitude of his mistake hit him.

Cyclops opened his X-Men communications channel for the first time in months. He spoke softly and quickly. Professor Xavier responded instantly.

"I will warn them, Cyclops. Thank you...and welcome back."

The professor's telepathic message came into people's minds, startling them at work, in school, on their way to the gym, in malls, everywhere.

They all heard it at the same time:

"I am Professor Xavier of the X-Men. You are in serious danger. Your city is about to be attacked. You must evacuate immediately. I have alerted the authorities and the military to help organize. Stay calm and you'll be all right. My students and I will do everything we can to protect you."

The professor hit hard, then lay still, waiting, his mental powers focused and ready. He saw Wolverine coming. Magneto didn't.

Professor Xavier strained to look up at his brother. "You can't do this," he said.

Magneto came closer. "Charles, you're a fool. Do you really think that by being weak you will somehow survive?"

The professor again tried to probe his brother's thoughts. He couldn't. The helmet was designed to protect Magneto from telepathy.

"This time you can't stop me," Magneto began, but Wolverine didn't give him the chance to finish.

"You're wrong about that," he hissed. "You're wrong about a lot of things."

"You can defeat me," Magneto rasped. "But the humans still won't get this planet. I'll destroy it."

For a split second, Wolverine didn't understand. Then the professor explained it to him. *He has armed every tactical nuclear missile in the world.* Wolverine hesitated, unsure what to do. If he attacked Magneto again, would he launch the missiles?

Quicksilver had followed his father, hoping, as always, to do something to make him proud. And, as always, his father was obsessed with his own power, nothing else.

It was hard to believe what Jean Grey was saying.

"Quicksilver?" she pleaded. "Did you here me? Magneto has armed all the tactical nuclear missiles on the planet."

Quicksilver knew in his heart it was true. His father would kill everyone in the world to prove how powerful he was...including his own son. It was time to make a terrible, painful decision. "I'm faster than anyone else." he said quietly.

A split second later, he was gone.

Quicksilver ran for his life—for everyone's life. He slowed as he neared his father, reaching out, timing it perfectly and removed Magneto's protective helmet.

Magneto tried to stand, but couldn't. How could this happen...defeated by a son who had never been anything but a pathetic failure? "Give me back the helmet," Magneto commanded.

Professor Xavier had been waiting for years for this chance.

The professor searched his brother's mind until he found what he was looking for. There. Magneto could control magnetic fields—that

Scraps of metal from the downed Sentinels leapt up like live things. Garbage cans, car bumpers, pieces of street signs and huge steel beams...every loose piece of metal in the city flew toward Magneto.

The professor knew what he had to do. If Magneto recovered, even for an instant, he'd fire the most terrible weapons man had ever made. Every person on Earth—mutant or normal—would be lost. In the name of humanity—*all* of humanity—that could not be allowed to happen. Professor Xavier lifted his brother through time and space. Finally, he found a suitable prison.

The professor had collapsed from the strain of defeating Magneto. The next few hours had been a tangle of voices, of helping hands. The X-Men had been there, all of them.

The president terminated the Sentinel program. Back at the school, Professor Xavier recovered; they all did.

"The X-Men have given the world a second chance," he told his students. "Be proud of what you have done." They were. But they knew they had a lifetime of work ahead of them. Still, standing among friends, they were full of hope.